JOE
on Sunday

Tony Blundell

DIAL BOOKS FOR YOUNG READERS

New York

For Karen, Oliver, and Joe

First published in the United States 1987 by
Dial Books for Young Readers
A Division of NAL Penguin Inc.
2 Park Avenue
New York, New York 10016

Published in Great Britain by
A & C Black (Publishers) Ltd.

Printed in Hong Kong by South China Printing Co.
First Edition
O B E
1 3 5 7 9 10 8 6 4 2

Library of Congress Cataloging-in-Publication Data
Blundell, Tony. Joe on Sunday.
Summary: Every day Joe seems to be someone
different as he behaves from dawn to dusk like
a pig, lion, mouse, monkey, monster, and king—
depending on how he feels.
[1. Behavior—Fiction.] I. Title.
PZ7.B6272Jo 1987   [E]   86-30944
ISBN 0-8037-0446-1

It was Sunday evening, and Joe was going to bed.

"Good night, Joe. See you in the morning."
"Good night, Mom," said Joe.

On Monday morning Joe's mom found . . .

a piggy in Joe's bed!

The piggy stuffed himself into Joe's clothes . . .

and gobbled up Joe's breakfast . . .

and his dad's breakfast too.
Then he went out to the garden and rolled in the mud.

After he had eaten his dinner . . .
and everyone else's . . .
he rolled in the mud again.

So the piggy had an early bath on Monday night.
He squealed and kicked the soap out of the bathtub.

"Good night, piggy," said Joe's mom. "See you in the morning."
"Grunt," said the piggy.

On Tuesday morning Joe's mom found . . .

a lion in Joe's bed.

The lion sprang into Joe's clothes . . .

and devoured Joe's breakfast in one enormous gulp.
Then he fell asleep on the couch.

For lunch he ate a dozen hamburgers
without any catsup.

With a mighty roar the lion pounced on Joe's dad . . .

and chewed up his slippers. Then he went to bed.

"Good night, lion," said Joe's mom. "See you in the morning."
"Prrrrrrr," said the lion.

On Wednesday morning Joe's mom found . . .

a tiny bump in Joe's bed.

"Squeak," peeped the little mouse . . .
and he wriggled into Joe's clothes.

He nibbled at Joe's breakfast.

Then he went to the supermarket in a basket . . .

and made a lady dance and shout.

The little mouse ate lots of cheese for lunch.
Then he built a nest under the cushions of the couch . . .

and hibernated.

That night he sailed Joe's boat around the bathtub.

"Good night, little mouse," said Joe's mom.
"See you in the morning."
"Squeak, squeak," peeped the little mouse, very quietly.

On Thursday morning Joe's mom found . . .

a monkey in Joe's bed.

The monkey put on Joe's clothes . . .

and juggled his breakfast.

Then he made faces at himself in the mirror.

The monkey went down to the park . . .

swung on the slide . . .

slid down the jungle bars . . .

and climbed on the swings.

In the evening he ate a banana or two . . .

then went to bed with a banana milk shake.

"Good night, monkey," said Joe's mom.
"See you in the morning."
"Eek, eek," squeaked the monkey.

On Friday morning Joe's mom found . . .
a monster in Joe's bed.

The monster ate up all of Joe's clothes . . .

and put on his breakfast.

Then he turned the living room upside down and . . .

danced around it.

He threw his lunch over the house . . .

and jumped rope with the clothesline.

The monster made huge waves in the bathtub.
Then he went to bed and gobbled up the pillow.

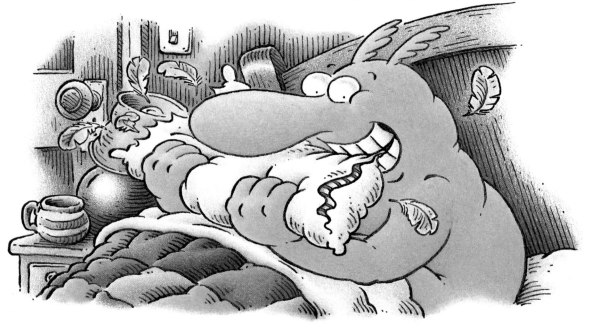

"Good night, monster," said Joe's mom.
"See you in the morning."
"Burp – delicious," belched the monster, spitting out feathers.

On Saturday morning, Joe's mom found . . .

a king in Joe's bed.
The king tried on all Joe's best robes.

Then he called for more
toast and honey . . .

and left all the bread crusts.

He rode around the shops in his carriage . . .

and had a mountain of ice cream for lunch.
In the afternoon he practiced being bossy . . .

and grumpy . . .

until he was very good at it.

That evening the king knighted Joe's teddies.

Then he demanded ten stories before he would go to bed.

"Good night, Your Majesty," said Joe's mom.
"See you in the morning."
"Hmmmmph," grumbled the grumpy king.

On Sunday morning Joe's mom found . . .

JOE.

Joe pulled on his clothes . . .

and ate a big breakfast.
Joe's mom and dad were very pleased to see him again.

They had a lovely day together.
That night Joe's mom tucked Joe into his bed.

"Good night, Joe," she said. "Will we see you in the morning?"
"Depends," said Joe. . . .

"It depends on what I feel like. . . .

Good night."